Fancy NANCY

Our Thanksgiving Banquet

Based on *Fancy Nancy* written by Jane O'Connor
Cover illustration by Robin Preiss Glasser
Interior illustrations by Lyn Fletcher and Beth Drainville

HARPER FESTIVAL
An Imprint of HarperCollinsPublishers

www.harpercollinschildrens.com
Library of Congress catalog card number: 2011901019
ISBN 978-0-06-123598-6
Graphic design by Sean Boggs
11 12 13 14 15   LEO   10 9 8 7 6 5 4 3 2 1 ❖ First Edition

Ooh *la la!* Grandma and Grandpa are hosting Thanksgiving dinner this year! After driving for hours, we have finally reached our destination—that's fancy for the place we want to be.

Grandpa opens the door and gives me a giant bear hug.

"Bonjour!" we both say. (My grandfather and I love to speak French to each other.)

What a celebration this will be! There is a gigantic turkey, Grandma's secret stuffing, green beans, and authentic cranberry sauce that didn't come out of a can. And desserts? There are almost too many to count.

This is not just a Thanksgiving dinner. This is way fancier. This is a Thanksgiving banquet!

When it is time to eat, I head for the big table.
My mom *tells* me to go sit at the kids' table—again!

"But I'm so much more mature than JoJo and my cousins," I say. (Mature is fancy for grown-up.)

"I know, but there aren't enough chairs at our table," Mom says.

I take my place at the kids' table. There are paper plates, paper napkins, and a paper tablecloth. The glasses are plastic. It is not nearly as fancy as the big table, but the food is simply delicious. I am careful to eat with my pinky up and, after each bite, I dab my lips with my napkin. That means I wipe my mouth very gently.

JoJo is not using her party manners! She puts her napkin on her head and makes silly faces. My cousin Arthur laughs so hard he spits out some cranberry juice.

My uncle has to intervene, which means he makes everyone stop acting so immature. "Would it be all right to switch seats with you?" he asks me. "Mais oui! Mais oui! Yes! Yes!" I tell him. "Of course!"

Grandma hands me a fresh napkin with a pretty holder around it.
You can wear it like a bracelet! Très chic! (You say it like this: tray sheek. It
means very fancy.)
And the gravy is passed around in a special little boat.

This is more like it.

I am ready for a second helping. I ask politely for the gravy boat. Oh, no! I spill a little by accident.

My grandma says, "I just spilled some cr[...]uce. Don't feel bad. That's what the tablecloth is for."

What a charming hostess my grandma is.

I finish eating way before anybody else. Have you noticed how long it takes grown-ups to eat? And how they only talk about stuff in the news?

"I can spell long words," I tell my aunt. "Like dazzle—d-a-z-z-l-e."
    "That's wonderful," my aunt says, but I can tell she is not really interested in spelling.

Ooh! JoJo and my cousins are already starting on dessert. My sister is having apple pie à la mode. (That's French and fancy for "with ice cream.")

JoJo waves to me and takes another bite of pie. "Yummy," she says.

Now everyone at the kids' table is coloring with the new crayons and pads of paper Grandma bought for us. Not to brag, but I am a very talented artist.

"May I be excused?" I ask Mom. I point to the kids' table. "I am going to help them draw stuff."

First I get a plate and sample the desserts.

Then I show everyone how to make butterflies.
(It's easy. You just make a big B together with another
big B that's backwards.)

Because it's Thanksgiving, I also teach them something I learned in school. You trace your hand, and—*voilà*—soon you have a turkey!

When we are done, we bring our turkeys over to the adults' table.

How to Make a Paper Turkey
1) Trace your hand.
2) Add feathers.
3) Add eyes and a beak.
4) Then fancy it up.
Voilà—a turkey!

"They are wonderful," Grandma and Grandpa tell us. They put the turkeys in the middle of the table, like a centerpiece.

Then Grandpa stands up and says how grateful (that's fancy for being happy and thankful) he is to have the whole family together.

Me, too. I'm so thankful for Thanksgiving.